THE WIND BLEW

THE WIND BLEW

PAT HUTCHINS

Red Fox

OTHER PICTURE BOOKS BY PAT HUTCHINS

Changes, Changes
Clocks and More Clocks
Don't Forget the Bacon!
The Doorbell Rang
Good-Night, Owl!
Happy Birthday, Sam
King Henry's Palace
One-Eyed Jake
One Hunter
Rosie's Walk
The Silver Christmas Tree
The Surprise Party
Titch
Tom and Sam
The Very Worst Monster
Silly Billy
Where's the Baby?
You'll Soon Grow into Them, Titch
Tidy Titch
My Best Friend

A Red Fox Book. Published by Random House Children's Books,
20 Vauxhall Bridge Road, London SW1V 2SA.
First published in Great Britain in 1974 by
The Bodley Head Children's Books
First published in paperback by Puffin 1978
Red Fox edition 1994.
Published in New York by Macmillan Publishing Co., Inc., 1974
© Pat Hutchins 1974
Printed in China
RANDOM HOUSE UK Limited Reg. No. 954009
ISBN 0 09 920751 6

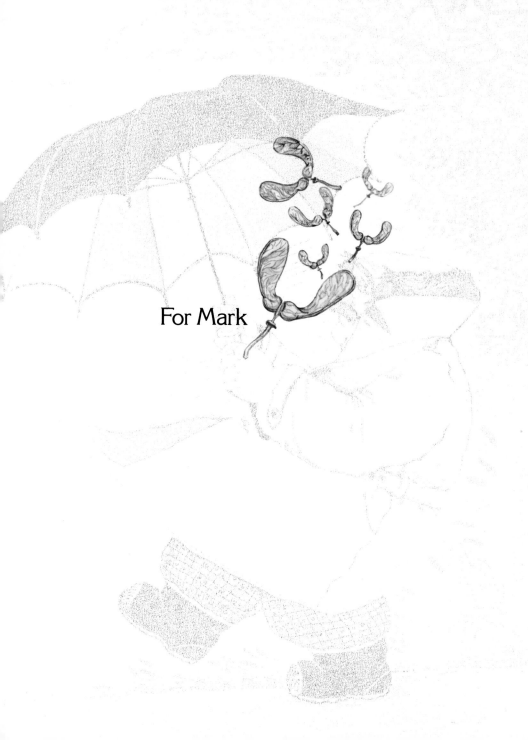

For Mark

The wind blew.

It took the umbrella from Mr. White
and quickly turned it inside out.

It snatched the balloon from little Priscilla
and swept it up to join the umbrella.

it snatched the balloon from little Priscilla
and swept it up to join the umbrella.

And not content, it took a hat,
and still not satisfied with that,

it whipped a kite into the air
and kept it spinning round up there.

It grabbed a shirt left out to dry
and tossed it upward to the sky.

It plucked a hanky from a nose
and up and up and up it rose.

It lifted the wig from the judge's head
and didn't drop it back. Instead

it whirled the postman's letters up,
as if it hadn't done enough.

It blew so hard it quickly stole
a striped flag fluttering on a pole.

It pulled the new scarves from the twins
and tossed them to the other things.

It sent the newspapers fluttering round,
then tired of the things it found,

it mixed them up

and threw them down

and blew away to sea.